The Camping Guy

By Dianne Greenlay

2

This is a work of fiction.

The names, characters, and incidents are products of the writer's imagination and are not to be construed as real. Any resemblance to persons living or dead is entirely coincidental.

Dedicated to Mike and Norm,
the original, unsurpassed Camping Guys.
And to Hazel,
for her spirit of a wonderfully fearsome bear.

Chapter One

It all started with a body part.

A fake one, as it turned out. Now perhaps some people wouldn't consider eyelashes to be a body part, but that's splitting hairs, isn't it?

What happened that day was a domino effect.

Oh, it didn't start out that way. It began, in fact, like any other day. My bedside alarm buzzed me awake at exactly 6:17 a.m. Twenty-three minutes later I was showered, dressed, and seated at my breakfast table, finishing the last delicious sips of my morning coffee, before I caught the 7:10 bus to the office.

Nothing in my routine was out of the ordinary. Just the way I liked it.

By mid morning, I was at my desk, sorting through a mound of a client's income tax papers, in preparation for his major audit, when his girlfriend dropped by. She looked just like what you'd expect for a petty mobster's girlfriend – buxom, tanned, and pretty in a heavily made-up sort of way.

But her very presence started warning bells ringing in my head. Her boyfriend's appointment wasn't until the end of the week. She was obviously there for dubious reasons, most likely, I thought, to attempt to use her feminine wiles to pressure me into falsifying something or other on his behalf.

She stopped at my desk, smiled, and leaned forward, spreading her perfectly manicured fingertips out on my desktop. I could only imagine the hand lotion fingerprints that she was leaving there.

She leaned even closer and her twin silicone mountains threatened to burst from their holders, so I (and rather wisely I thought,) focused intently on her face. On her eyes, to be exact. And that's when it happened.

The body part let loose.

No, not one of the wiggly, jiggly, silicone parts. The eyelash strip. One end just sort of sprang up from the inner corner of her eye, and every time she blinked, it bobbed, still tethered to one end of her eyelid, flapping like a miniature windshield washer. It was mesmerizing in a peculiar sort of way.

"What's wrong with your eye?" I asked, without giving careful consideration or thought as to the possible consequences of such an inquiry.

Well, she touched her eyelid and discovered the errant body part.

Embarrassed, she screeched in alarm.

My heart jumped right into the fray, pounding in even greater alarm as the reality of my sudden predicament washed over me: I had inadvertently distressed the mobster's girlfriend.

My stress levels soared.

Her initial screech threatened to build into a full-bodied wail and my guts suddenly clenched in a fierce and untimely response to my fiber-heavy breakfast.

I bolted from my cubicle, spilling my coffee all over my desktop.

Grabbing my business magazine, I rescued it from this soggy flood, and sought safe refuge in the men's washroom, intending to be in there for quite some time. Or at least until she left.

As I said, it was the domino effect.

Positioned quite comfortably, I waited for all of my body systems to calm down and to do what they were designed to do. In the meantime, I opened my magazine, and that's when I saw the ad.

Executive De-stressing. Get away from it all.
Guided one-on-one wilderness camping.
Our motto is "If you're not living on the edge,
You're taking up TOO MUCH ROOM!"
Call Earl – the Camping Guy!

So I did, and I signed up on the spot. I'd never been camping before. I was really looking forward to it and Earl – well, Earl, he was quite the guy.

Chapter Two

I have to say that Earl inspired confidence right from the start.

It was kind of infectious, really. The man was rugged-looking in his jeans, vest, and hiking boots. Fierce, even. And he wore a dangerous looking knife strapped to his belt. He oozed self-assurance from every pore.

Our wilderness adventure began with a hike in the mountains. To where? I dunno. Mostly straight up. It seemed like hours later that I vaguely heard him calling my name from somewhere ahead of me. I couldn't see him, bent over as I was by the unaccustomed weight of a backpack.

"Johnson! Johnson!" Earl's voice cut through the still mountain air.

"I'm here," I replied, puffing so hard that I sounded like I was having a full blown asthma attack.

"Oh. I couldn't see you behind that bush."

"I'm somewhat closer to the ground than I was when we started," I pointed out, struggling, without much success, to straighten up.

Earl bent over and studied the ground. "What are you looking at?"

"I'm not looking at anything," I replied with more frustration showing through than I had intended.

"I just don't think that I can straighten up. When you offered to set up this camping weekend, I never suspected it would turn into an endurance trek for Sherpas!"

"It's all in your attitude, my boy," Earl reprimanded me. "You know, the thing about hiking is that half of it is about 90 per cent mental."

I was a little perplexed. "Is that new math?"

Earl ignored my dilemma completely and continued. "Well, don't just stand there. Let's get started. Heave that Nerf pack off, my man, and let's christen this place!"

Easily said. Not easily done.

That pack stuck to me like fuzz on Velcro and my frantic attempts to remove it only succeeded in causing me to lose my balance. I fell to my knees, rolled onto my side, and ended up on my back, extended over the pack.

There I was, stuck like a turtle, belly up, while Earl, oblivious to my plight, dug out two small bottles of Scotch from his pack and emptied each one into a couple of mugs that he seemed to have produced from thin air. He turned to hand one to me and seemed surprised at my new position.

"You do yoga, Johnson?" he asked.

"No," I replied, "but it's not a bad idea. Give me a hand would you?"

Earl reached out and wrestled that pack off my back in no time flat, leaving me feeling like I'd just been skinned. Boy, was I ready for that drink. We both perched our butts on a couple of large flat rocks and sipped our Scotch. I can't say that I'd ever drunk any liquid out of a tin mug before. I supposed that this was the first stage of roughing it.

I looked around, taking in the quiet majesty of the mountains that surrounded us. I breathed the crisp, fresh air, which was devoid of any city smog and odor. It was amazing. There was no drone of traffic, no shouting of harried pedestrians, no hum of electronics or machinery. It was absolute peace. I could feel my blood pressure dropping by the minute.

After a bit, my curiosity got the better of me. "So how come you decided that *this* is the place to stop? What qualities did this particular piece of land exhibit? Did it speak to you, in your heart? Was it this high spot, overlooking virgin forest?"

Earl stared at me, not answering. He was probably completely astonished, I thought, at my astute level of comprehension with regards to his motivation. I continued, warming to my deductive reasoning.

"Or maybe you looked around and saw an abundance of natural resources!" I was sure that I was on to something.

"Shrubs for shelter from the wind, trees for shade, a river nearby to wash in, a rocky clearing here so a campfire won't get away on you. Was that it, Earl?"

"No."

"Well, why'd you stop here? What makes this place different from that 'meeting place' that you pointed out to me back down the trail a bit – you know, the place where that pile of rocks was, where we're supposed to head to if we become separated. Why did you pick *this* particular place?"

Earl shrugged. "Got tired of walking."

"Oh," I replied. I could see right away that Earl was a man of few words, and one who filled his world with simple choices. I envied that. We sipped our Scotch in silence.

Earl finished his drink first and stood up. "Now Johnson, listen carefully. First business on the agenda: I am going to tell you how to set up a full fly tent."

"Full fly?" I had never heard of such a thing.

"Yep." Earl pulled a bright blue wad of nylon material from his pack and unrolled it. "This is the beauty of a full fly, Johnson. It allows a guy to set up his tent in the rain and the inside of the tent won't get wet so you can keep your packs dry. It's very expensive but it's worth it."

"Even if it doesn't rain?" I asked.

Earl shot me a pained look. "Well no, Johnson, if it doesn't rain, then you don't need a full fly."

My unerring sense of logic roared to life. "So, if you have one, you gotta' hope for rain, right?"

"What?"

I couldn't believe that I was going to have to explain this to him. "Well, I don't know that much about camping, but hoping for rain when you're camping doesn't make much sense to me, so based on that, I can only conclude that using a full fly is not a good thing."

Perhaps I had overestimated him. He seemed not to follow. His eyebrows pulled together in a deep frown. "Just set up the tent, Johnson."

"One question before I do."

"What's that?"

I looked at the pile of blue nylon at my feet. "Well, what *is* a full fly anyway?"

Earl stared at me for a long moment before speaking. "Maybe *I* should set up the tent. We won't need a fly today, anyway. *You* hang a clothesline up over there somewhere, OK, Johnson?"

He withdrew a coil of rope from his pack and tossed it to me. "Just string this piece of rope between two trees in a sunlit place so wet things will dry."

Pleased to be contributing in some fashion, I chatted on, eager to be engaging him in conversation and all the while trying to disentangle the rope. "You know, Earl, I feel intuitively that you are an above average camper and you know, to be above average is a good thing, because, well, half the people in the world are below average, so it's a good thing to be in the top half."

Earl gave a happy sounding snort. "Sort of like sleeping two to a hammock. You want to be on the top half, right?"

I frowned. "I don't think I ever slept in a hammock."

"It was a *joke*, Johnson! Use your imagination!"

"Oh."

I thought hard for a moment, building a picture in my mind. "Hey, Earl! I'm imagining two in a hammock and it's me and Pamela Anderson, naked as jaybirds, and in this case it's not necessarily a bad thing to be on the bottom."

Earl allowed a small slip of a smile to slide across his face. "Stay on task, Johnson," he commanded, in an official tone. "Besides doing the clothesline, you can set out the food in one pile, and the cooking pots and utensils in another."

Jeez Louise! Humor wasn't this guy's strong suit. He continued to pound stakes into the ground and very quickly erected our tent and placed our sleeping bags in it.

I took inventory of our cooking supplies. A mesh bag with a small burner. One large pot. Numerous foil packages. I ran out of hands to hold things with, so I put the pot on my head and examined the foil packages. They contained several varieties of dehydrated food.

"Where do you want these items, exactly?" I asked.

Earl looked over at me and laughed. "You look like a Kamikaze pilot!"

Ah-ha! The man did have a funny bone after all. I grinned and pointed to the pot. "This is my full-fly helmet! Keeps the rain off!"

Earl just shook his head and then waved his hand at the food packages. "We'll put that stuff on the far side of the clothesline after we eat. We want to keep food away from the tent."

"Huh?" I had been momentarily lost in thought. "Oh, sorry. I was just wondering, why *would* a Kamikaze pilot wear a helmet?"

Earl's scowl was back. "Stay on task, Johnson. On task. Food, and anything that has contact with food, eventually goes over yonder."

On task. There was that phrase again. Earl was indeed going to be a hard task master. I tried to lighten the mood. "Don't want to go to sleep smelling like smoked pork chops, eh?"

"There's nothing a bear would like better than two tasty, pork-smelling man-wiches pre-wrapped in sleeping bags. We'll hang everything from a tree far away from the tent."

Man, what a stickler for boring details! I read the labels on the packages of dehydrated foods. "What is this stuff? 'Just add a half of a cup of boiling water to bag and let sit three minutes. Serve hot.' Well, I guess it *would* be hot if it's got boiling water in it."

Earl grabbed the foil packages out of my hands. "Four Cheese Lasagna. Beef Stroganoff. Strawberry Cheesecake. Beer Reconstitute. Everything a guy could want!"

"Beer Reconstitute? Made with water?" I was curious. "Would that be light beer then?"

"Hardly!" Earl seemed affronted. "People who drink light beer don't even like the taste of beer. They only like to pee a lot. See, it also gives 'em exercise getting up and down to pee." He bounced up and down, doing a series of deep knee bends.

"If I squatted up and down like that when I peed, I'd never hit the toilet bowl!" I exclaimed. It made my knees ache just to watch him.

"I was referring to an entire evening of urination, Johnson. I was compressing it into one short vignette."

"Vignette? Of peeing? Now there's a novel concept for a CBC production. Hey, speaking of peeing, where *is* the bathroom?" I hadn't seen any washrooms along the way.

"Well, there aren't exactly any man-made facilities out here. You just sort of dig a hole, back-a-ways in the bush, and do your business there. And you can always pee in the river when you're swimming."

"Ah!" I pondered this. More roughing it. Well it wasn't going to be so haphazard, if I could help it. "Just so long as *I'm* the guy upstream," I warned, "because what's acceptable to the guy upstream is not necessarily acceptable to the guy downstream, right?"

"Right!"

"So," I continued, "if I'm swimming in the river and you're in there too, and the water suddenly gets warm, it had better be a thermal fissure from the river bottom that I'm experiencing!"

Earl shot me a grumpy look. "Yeah, yeah, don't obsess about your water works. Let's get ready to get a fire going. You gather kindling and I'll get some firewood."

Jeez Louise! I still hadn't hung up the clothesline and already he was giving me another task. The hike up here had really given me an appetite and I was looking forward to even a simple cup of tea but I could tell that Earl, in his own way, was a very orderly person. It was going to be first things first. I picked up the rope and stepped into the bushes, looking for an appropriate spot to install the clothesline.

It didn't take me very long to decide upon two saplings. I secured each end of the rope to a thin trunk using the same kind of knot that I always used in my bowling shoes. I gathered a few dried branches and twigs that littered the ground, to use as kindling, and then returned to our apparent camping spot.

I hadn't been gone that long but what greeted me when I got back there was a horrible sight.

Chapter Three

Some unidentified animal covered in striped fur was *attacking Earl and had attached itself to his head!*

My latent survival reflexes kicked in and I grabbed a two-foot long log and sprang to Earl's defense. A primal howl ripped from my throat as I launched my own attack. With one well-aimed smash, I knocked the critter from Earl's head, and just in time too, it seemed, as Earl immediately collapsed to the ground. A few more swings of my log left only a furry carcass beaten into the ground.

"What the hell was *that*?" I wheezed and gasped, and poked at the carcass with my log.

Earl struggled to his knees, clasping his bleeding forehead. Thank God the man was still conscious. He stared at the pummeled lump on the ground, apparently still in shock. Finally he spoke.

"It used to be my raccoon-tail hat."

"Your what? Oh! I am *so* sorry! When I turned around and saw some sort of *animal* in what appeared to be a death grip on your scalp, well, I was just *consumed* with panic. Who would get us out of here and home safe and sound if something were to happen to you?"

Blood trickled down his forehead and Earl wiped at it with the back of his hand. "Felt that beating me unconscious with that log was the lesser of two evils, did you?"

"It was the only weapon I had at hand," I pointed out the obvious. The man was so ungrateful! I had just potentially saved his life and there he was, responding with sarcasm.

"Thank God *I'm* the one that had the axe," he said.

A childish response, I thought. Still, one of us had to be the adult here. "Look, I'm really sorry. Here! Let me bandage you up." I looked in my pack and withdrew my first-aid kit. I lined up a small bottle, a gauze pad, and a band-aid.

"No, really Johnson, it's OK. It's not that bad." It seemed that Earl was going to play the tough guy role.

"No, no," I insisted. "I didn't want to come on this trip completely unprepared, you know, so I packed a few things of my own. I have just the stuff to take care of that head wound! How's your sight by the way?"

"My sight? Other than being a little blurry from the *blood* dripping in my eye, it's fine! Why?"

"I just wanted to make sure you didn't have double vision. I read in my first aid manual that double vision is a very bad sign."

Earl squinted up at me. "Yeah, I can understand how seeing *two of you* would cause a man to panic."

I chose to ignore his barb. He was obviously a little emotionally unstable from his head injury.

"Here. Hold still." I poured a splash of the fluid from the bottle onto the gauze pad and dabbed at his cut.

In a split second, Earl exploded to his feet. "What in the hell is *that* stuff?" he screeched.

"My aftershave. I couldn't find the antibiotic cream so I improvised." I read the label. "Aftershave has twenty-five per cent alcohol in it."

Earl continued to hop around and hold his head. "*Jesus! That burns! And smells!*" he roared.

I sniffed at the gauze pad. "Well, it might be a little out of date and perhaps a tiny bit rancid. Hold still now," I scolded. "Here comes the bandage."

Earl was still bouncing around a bit and I wasn't happy with its initial placement. "Wait a minute," I cautioned. "It's not covering the whole cut." I ripped the tape off with one swift pull.

Earl howled again. "*My eyebrow!* You've pulled my entire eyebrow out by the roots!"

I examined the hairy band-aid and decided to get a fresh one."Just a few hairs, that's all. What's a few hairs? Your eyebrows are entirely too bushy anyways. Here, hold still!"

This time Earl reluctantly co-operated.

"There. All done," I soothed. I stepped back and looked at him. "You know, with that band-aid in place, no one will even notice that you have only one eyebrow." I dusted my hands off, pleased that the band-aid had worked. My stomach suddenly growled as if to grab my attention. "Let's have a nice cup of tea, shall we?" I asked.

"What about my hat?" Earl persisted. "I feel naked without my hat!"

His hat? This was annoying. Earl was still obsessing about his hat. Humoring him, I peered at his thinning hair. "While not exactly naked, I would agree that you *are* moderately follically challenged."

"What the hell does that mean?"

"You have entered that certain stage of life. The *trade-off* zone," I explained.

"The what?"

"Everything's a trade-off from here on. The waistline thickens, as the hair thins. The hair on your head doesn't grow much, but it sprouts endlessly from your ears and nostrils. I tell you, it's a trade-off. Blood pressure goes up, erec –"

"OK, OK, I get the picture!" Earl interrupted. "It's depressing! I'm not looking forward to getting any older!"

He needed some cheering up. I hit him with the time-honored one liner. "I always think that it's OK to get older, just so long as you don't get *old*!"

"A fine but important distinction," Earl huffed. He picked up his hat. "Look at my hat! What am I going to use now?"

The hat again. Earl was definitely verging on having an episode of a previously undiagnosed obsessive-compulsive disorder. I offered a solution. "I'll lend you one of mine."

"*One* of yours? How many did you bring?"

"Three. This one here," I pointed to the one that I was already wearing, "is for sunshine. It's vented and has a wide brim for shade." I dug around in my pack and produced my Sou'westerner. "This one is for rain because it's coated with some sort of rubbery stuff, and this one," I continued as I held up my knitted toque, "is a spare for whatever. It has chin ties and this little tufty thing on top." I put it on Earl, tying it on securely.

"Very good in the wind," I pointed out. "It's like a little wind sock." I gave the tassels a flick with my fingers. "See, you can tell which way the wind is blowing. And look, this one," I referred back to the one which I wore, "has compartments inside the lining, to store things in – a hand wipe, money, keys – whatever you want."

Earl untied the toque. "But that's what pockets in your pants are for."

Oh Lord, I thought, grant me patience. I furthered the obvious. "But suppose you change your pants and forget to transfer all the stuff? I bet you don't change your hat as often as you change your pants, do you?" I challenged. Earl seemed to be thinking this over. "And one day, there they'd be, all the emergency things you need, right in your hat, regardless of what pants you're wearing."

"I see," Earl remarked. "Every home should have one."

"Definitely. You can borrow one of these hats anytime that you want." He couldn't claim that I hadn't tried to help. "Now about that tea."

Earl crouched down and gathered the kindling, placing it in a pile to one side. "We won't light a fire just yet," he explained. "Bring the mini-burner over, would you?" I handed it to him and watched closely as he set it up. "Using this to boil water is faster than building a fire to do it, but it's still tedious. Bring those mugs over here and get the tea bags out of your pack, too, Johnson."

I handed him the tea bags that I had packed in a small clear plastic bag. Earl held up the bag and his brows knitted together. "What the hell? Your teabags have gone moldy, Johnson!"

"Moldy? Let me see!" A wave of relief washed over me. "That's not mold, that's powdered milk!"

"Powdered milk?"

"Yes. You see, I like a spot of milk with my tea so I thought, why not wet them and then batter the tea bags with powdered milk crystals?"

"Batter them?" Earl looked bewildered.

"Yes," I explained. "That way when I use them to make tea, I'll have tea *and* milk, all in one cup." It had been a brilliant idea, in my opinion.

Earl seemed to be coming around to my way of thinking because he only shook his head and laughed. "I'd hate to see what you'd do with bacon and eggs!"

He wet one finger and held it up, testing the wind direction. There was barely a breeze, but I suppose he was showing off a bit. "Here, hold this shield around the burner and kind of block the breeze while I light it." He handed me a piece of aluminum foil that had been folded over several times to make a stiff eight-inch square.

I held it as he had directed but it blocked my line of sight and learning how to make a fire was one survival skill that I didn't want to miss even one detail of. I tilted the shield back slightly so that I could better see Earl's technique. "How do you do that? I can't really see what you're doing."

"*Yeow!*" Earl fell back, flicking his right hand and began to yell again. "You have to hold the shield *still*, Johnson! Otherwise the fire shifts direction and *people get hurt!*"

Jeez Louise! What a hot head! I was beginning to feel that it was unlikely that we would reach the male bonding stage at all on this trip.

"Sorry!" I said. "I just wanted to see how you did this for when it's my turn to heat things up."

Earl was gritting his teeth and still shaking his hand about. "Johnson, *you* seem to be able to heat things up without a flame!"

"Let me get the first aid kit," I offered.

"No-o-o!" Earl exclaimed. "No more first aid, thanks. Here, let me do this. You stand over by the bushes and break wind there." I stood a few feet away, trying in vain to see what he was doing. At last he spoke. "Hand me a water bottle."

I was relieved. Time to do something useful again. I handed the bottle to him and he emptied it into the pot that he had placed on top of the burner, and then he smiled.

And there we were. Just like that. Partners performing a basic survival technique. I was kind of proud of that and was a little bit surprised that it had come so naturally to me.

I inhaled deeply, enjoying this sensation of a lungful of clean air. I stepped nearer to Earl. "You know, I think I could really catch on to this camping."

Earl was focused on coaxing the water to boil and seemed to be much more relaxed than he had been a few minutes earlier. Our buddy moment had worked some kind of magic.

"You just need the right basic gear and it can be entirely civilized," he remarked. "Maybe you and your wife will take it up together sometime."

"Gladys? No, I don't think so. If there's one thing, no, two things – two things that my wife doesn't like, it's the wilderness and athletics, and there is a high concentration of both in camping, it seems."

"What about the beauty of the flowers in the daytime and the gentle gurgling of the creek, lulling you to sleep at night?"

Boy, Earl could be pretty poetic when he wanted to be.

"No," I replied. "The flowers make her sneeze and they attract bugs, she thinks, and the gurgling would be akin to me keeping her awake at night with my snoring. No, she wouldn't like it. And she'd feel claustrophobic in a tent, too."

Earl glanced up from his burner. "Doesn't like close spaces, eh?"

I sat down on the rock's smooth surface. This was going to be a conversation that was much too long to have standing up. "No, she doesn't. You know, one time we went to Mexico on a holiday, and in a moment of weakness, Gladys said she'd come with me on a snorkel trip down into an underground lake that was in this big cave.

"Well, we're floating away, life jackets, flippers, and snorkels on, and we're about fifteen minutes into it, when Gladys spies a chimney of light about this big around, in the ceiling of the cave that we're in, and the next thing I know, she's making like a mountain climber, scaling up the wall of the cave, flippers and all, headed towards this hole in the ceiling."

"She couldn't stand being in the cave anymore?" Earl asked.

"No, she couldn't, and although I don't believe that ceiling shaft was originally big enough to escape through, Gladys was like a cat that thinks that if it can get its head through a tight space, its body will follow. Yessir, I believed she actually pioneered an exit that day with her bare hands!"

Earl chuckled at the mental picture I'd just painted. "Well, camping *is* better off being a guy thing," he said. "The ladies are often too delicate. Although," he paused, probably for theatrical effect I thought, because he then touched his eyebrow and squinted at his burned hand, "*some* trips can be more dangerous than others!"

"Danger. Hmm. Yes!" I nodded in agreement. "That's why I thought this trip would be the perfect opportunity to learn the art of camping. Especially with an expert like yourself in charge. Do you do a lot of camping?"

Earl was suddenly subdued. I'd struck a nerve somehow. He was quiet for what seemed like forever, and then he glanced at me. "Used to camp the whole year round. Now I only go out a couple of times each summer, mostly when I have clients like yourself along."

"Why is that?" I asked. "I mean, you have all of this equipment. Seems a shame to waste it. You'd think you'd be out using it as often as you could."

"Yeah, well, circumstances change ...." Earl's voice trailed off.

After a few moments more of uncomfortable silence, I tried to get the conversation going again. "So, how long have you had your camping business?"

"I started it about two years ago."

I nudged him some more. "Is that why you have all this equipment?" At first he didn't answer. I wondered why he was being so evasive. I pushed him again. "Well, is it?"

Earl heaved a big sigh. "No, I had most of it before." He stared at me as if deciding whether or not to take me into his confidence.

He pursed his lips together and then continued, but now his voice wavered and I felt a flutter of alarm grow in my chest. This big mountain man's voice cracked. "You see, I used to go camping and hiking with my son. A lot. Then he got sick. Really sick."

Earl's voice dropped. "Aggressive leukemia, the doctors called it." He closed his eyes. "I would have given my own life in exchange for his."

Hearing this forced confession, I suddenly felt sick, like I'd been punched in the gut. Me and my big mouth.

Earl blinked hard and clenched his jaw, regaining control. "He was just twelve years old when he passed away." He paused again.

"I didn't come up to these mountains for a long time after that ... but ... life goes on, and these mountains were still here, waiting for me. Calling for me. So I started coming up again, and you know

I always feel better when I'm up here. I feel the peace of nature all around me. It's like my son's spirit is still with me ... up here."

Oh. My. God.

I had pried until, for a brief moment, the crack in Earl's soul had split wide open. Nothing I said now could make either of us feel any worse, so I simply said what I was thinking.

"You know, I think that your son would have liked that you still come up into these mountains. He would have liked that you're carrying on the tradition."

Earl nodded, his hard veneer sliding into place again. "I like to believe that, too." He went quiet once more. The minutes ticked by.

I had to break the painful silence. "Uh, is that water ready?" I pointed at the burner.

Earl seemed grateful for the change of topic. "I suppose it's near enough." He poured water into both mugs and I slipped one of my milk-coated teabags into each one.

"There! Instant tea with a splash of milk!" I exclaimed.

Earl peered into his mug and smiled back at me. "Well, I'll be damned. It worked."

"Cheers!" I toasted.

"Cheers." Earl swallowed a big sip of tea and then said, "I thought we'd maybe fry up a couple of fish for supper."

"You brought fish?" I asked delightedly.

"No, Johnson, we have to catch them first. We'll fish. In the river."

"Hey!" I responded. "That would be great! Do you know, other than netting out my goldfish when I want to clean their aquarium, I don't believe I have ever actually caught a fish."

"Goldfish in a tank don't count. I brought along a few worms to use as bait. Let's get the rod out. Here we go."

He passed two pieces of rod to me and fiddled with a small wriggling worm and a dangerous looking hook that was decorated with some brightly colored whiskery strands.

"See, you have to make sure the worm is securely on the hook. Otherwise the fish can nibble it off and get away."

"OK. Let me try," I said. I wasn't keen on handling the worm so I let Earl continue to hold it while I attempted to spear it with the hook. "This worm's pretty adept at worm gymnastics," I chuckled. "Hold still you little bugger!" I pushed quick and hard. "There!"

"*Ouch!*" Earl yelled.

"What's the matter?"

"You seem to have impaled *my finger!*"

Jeez Louise! Earl was sure accident prone. "Oh? Let me look. You're right. But look! I got the worm on the hook, too."

"Thank God the barb is not through," Earl observed. "I think I can pull it out."

Oh no! I had just gotten that worm on the hook and he was about to undo my handiwork. "Don't let the worm off!" I warned. "It has to stay on the hook. Don't let it drop on the ground! Where else would we put it?"

Earl frowned at me. "I know where *I'd* like to put it!"

He continued to disengage the hook from his finger, while I, unnoticed by him, came to his rescue again. I took off my hat and removed a small vial from the lining.

"There we are!" Earl held his finger up to examine it and I saw my opportunity. I splashed the contents of the vial on Earl's fingertip.

"Hey! What're you doing? *Christ, that burns!* What the hell is *that?*"

"Same stuff. My aftershave." I held up the vial. "Travel size bottle. Part of the emergency supplies, like I told you. Fits quite nicely in the hat," I bragged. I tucked the vial back into my hat's lining.

"Now your finger won't develop some sort of weird worm infection, because it's been disinfected! Wouldn't want you developing blood poisoning or something, because without you here to guide me, well, there's no telling how much trouble I'd be in."

Earl sucked his fingertip and gagged. "Jeez! It *tastes* worse than it smells!" He glared at me. "Did your mother ever *encourage* you to run with scissors?"

My mother? Now he was inquiring about my background? I assumed that he was impressed with my first aid skills and probably thought that there was a family inclination towards the medical profession.

"No," I replied."Funny thing, that. I was an only child and my parents kept all the knives and scissors in a locked drawer, even when I was older." I shrugged. "Just being unnecessarily protective of their only offspring, I guess."

Earl ran his hands over his face. "Well, maybe we'll save the fishing lesson until tomorrow. I've kinda' lost my enthusiasm for it right now."

What? I didn't want to lose any opportunity for another wilderness lesson. "Enthusiasm? This is not a pep rally!" I exclaimed. "We don't have to do cartwheels! This is just fishing. You just plunk the hook in the water and wait for a fish to come by, don't you?"

"Absolutely not!" he retorted. Obviously, I had affronted him. Earl grabbed the pieces of the rod and slid them together. "Fishing is a fine art! A practiced, highly polished technique –"

"Wait!" I interrupted. "This is not gold smithing we're talking about. What the hell do you polish on a fish?"

Caught again in his wild exaggeration, Earl seemed exasperated. "It's a figure of speech! You see, with fishing, there's a fine line between fishing," and he mimicked casting the rod, "and just standing in the water up to your crotch, looking like an idiot."

"So," I tried to sort this out in my mind, "you mean to say that if you and I were standing in the river together and someone saw us, they would be hard pressed to tell which one was fishing and which one was the idiot?"

My logic had clearly beaten him. Earl just shook his head and said, "Don't even ask."

"Well if we're not going to eat fish, how about we try out those dehydrated meals? I'm starving." My metabolism was clearly not used to all of this exercise.

"OK. Think you can handle getting a pot full of water from the river? I'll go down the hill a-ways, pick out a good sturdy tree, and put up a rope so that we can hoist our packs up in the air later on this evening. We don't want the bears getting at them."

"What we need is a dog," I offered.

"We don't need a dog."

"Yes we do. For a sort of an alarm system. You know. Barking at intruders. Sounding the alarm." I gave my best dog bark-and-howl imitation.

"Johnson, did you know that dogs are just as likely to *attract* bears? Especially if they're tied up?"

"Why would we tie a dog up? It's not like there's any neighbor's lawn to crap on up here." I was no Star Trek Spock, but in comparison to me,

Earl's thought processes were completely devoid of any logic.

"National park rules. All pets must be leashed. And kept quiet."

"We are ten thousand miles straight up from nowhere. Who would hear?"

"*I* would. I don't like noise much. That's *why* I camp up here. No noise!" he yelled.

Boy, it didn't take much to set him off shouting again. "Alright," I said. "So you're going to rope a tree or something like that and I am going to the river, right?"

"Right. There's a collapsible container in one of those packs that you can dig out." Earl grabbed two pieces of rope from a pocket on his backpack. "Here's a piece of rope for you to tie onto the container so that you can haul it out of the river. I'll use this one to make a pack pulley in a tall tree." He spun on his heels and stomped away.

I watched Earl leave, striding out of sight. "Earl! Earl!" I called, but got no response. The trees seemed to be closing in around me. I called more frantically and louder.

"*Earl!*"

A loud crashing in the bushes told me that he had finally heard me.

"What?" he yelled, just before he burst out of the bushes and tripped on the log that I had used to save his life with only a few short hours ago.

"*Ye-ow-w!*" He slammed into a heap on the ground.

"Oh my God! Are you alright, Earl?" I tried to pull him onto his feet.

"Don't touch me! Ow! I think I've bruised my shoulder. What were you yelling about anyway?"

How could I explain the reassurance that I, a camping neophyte, needed from him, my woodsman hero? "I just wanted to know – how long will you be gone?"

Earl stared at me. "The entire time, Johnson."

"Oh."

It was kind of tough to read his expression and he didn't stick around at all anyway. With his rope in one hand, and holding his bruised shoulder with the other, Earl limped away into the bushes once more and I didn't dare call him back for more clarification.

I began to search through the pack to look for the container. I made a mental list of the items as I came upon them. Pajamas. Extra long johns. Warm shirt. Weird plastic bag full of ... bacon! My poor stomach growled again. That bacon was going to be terrific for breakfast.

I tossed the items one by one into the tent until I eventually found the collapsible water container. "This must be it! Rope! Water container! Down to the river we go!"

Foolishly cheerful, I had no idea of the experience that awaited me there.

Chapter Four

I staggered back into our campsite clearing, teeth chattering and hands stiff from the paralyzing cold of the river.

There you are!" Earl snatched the container from my hand, not bothering to take note of my wet and bedraggled condition, but staring only at the three inches of water that sloshed about in the container. "Why did you bring back only two cupfuls, Johnson?"

"Well, I had some trouble at the river – fell in, as a matter of fact – and as you can see, this container has only a little tiny hole for the water to go in, and not much did."

"Did what?"

"Went in."

"Do you know how to burp a container, Johnson?" Earl's eyebrows lifted, in what I thought was genuine curiosity.

"Burp a container? No. I burped my wife's niece's baby once. Put her on her tummy over my knees and patted her gently on the back. She threw up all over my shoes."

Earl sighed. "You have a real way with babies and grown-ups alike, don't you, Johnson? Well, let's get started with the water that you do have. Where's your rope?"

Ugh. It was time to confess. "Uh ... actually, I lost it in the river. Saved the container, though!"

Earl's face flushed and he growled. "That was our last piece of spare rope! I sure hope we aren't gonna' regret not having it."

I already did. There was nothing left to hang myself with to end this experience. "This camping thing is new for me, Earl. Really new. You have to assume I know nothing and proceed from there."

Earl only nodded. "That's kinda' what I *was* thinking, Johnson. In fact, I came out here with *no* expectations as to your abilities, and so far, well, let's just say, I haven't been disappointed."

"Great!" I felt a warm flood of relief. Earl was not going to yell at me again. However, I was going to need more sustenance than just his approval to make it through the night. I spied the food packages. "Well, what should we have?"

Earl picked up the foil packages. "How about the lasagna?" He waved another package in front of me. "Beef?"

"Maybe." I was so hungry I couldn't decide.

"Turkey with Dumplings?"

My stomach was just about turning inside out with hunger. "How about we try them all?"

"C'mon," Earl said. "Choose one."

"No, seriously," I insisted. "Let's have a smorgasbord!"

"Yeah? And what will we eat tomorrow?"

"Leftovers!" I exclaimed. "Turkey *always* tastes better the second day."

Earl shook his head. "Do you have any idea how long it would take to boil enough water to make *all* of these?"

Where there was a will, there was a way. "We could snack on the first one while the water boils for the second one and so on."

I could see Earl was considering it. "They *do* look good in the pictures, don't they? Well, to hell with the diet! Which one first?"

"Apple pie!"

"Apple pie? That's dessert!"

Again I used simple logic. "It all ends up in your stomach at the end of a meal, doesn't it? I don't think it stays layered in the order in which it's been eaten. I think that it makes *no* difference at all. Besides, this way we won't be too full for dessert!"

I felt a certain degree of accomplishment when Earl suddenly laughed and said, "What the hell. We *are* camping, after all. Yeah! We can eat *what* we want, *when* we want, *if* we want! We can nap the afternoon away, and we *don't* have to shower or shave –"

I jumped to my feet. "Or wear deodorant or change our underwear if *we don't want to! Yeah!*"

We grinned at each other with a matching look of triumph on our faces for a moment, and then Earl frowned. "Well, maybe the underwear thing is a little much, Johnson ... it *is* a small tent after all."

I felt a little giddy now that I had started to thaw out but no way was I going to let 'Surly Earl' dampen my enthusiasm. "Damn! I feel so alive, so free! I am going to take these clothes off, right now!" I started to unbuckle my belt.

"Hey! Whoa, there good buddy! That's not such a good idea!" Earl grabbed for my hand but missed by a fraction of an inch, wedging his fingers into my waistband instead. I dropped my gaze to his hand.

"Neither is that!"

Well, unflappable Earl became kind of flustered. "Ah, that is to say, yes, sorry about that, I only meant, that it's not a very good idea to bare much skin up here because ... because of the no-see-ums! Yes! That's right. Nasty little mouths on flies that bite! Gladys wouldn't want you returning with Mr.

Happy and the Boys all bitten and swollen up, now would she?"

Mr. Happy? It took me a moment to realize that this was guy-talk. Pure testosterone. Earl was introducing me to the world of man-speak! It was the primal topics and the rough language that guys used to converse with when the ladies were out of earshot. I was being initiated. I had to 'cowboy up', as the saying went.

"You know, Earl," I tried to sound more masculine than I felt, "I haven't had the mouth of anything down there since my honeymoon!" There! I'd done it. "But still, I see your point. I *don't* think I'd like to hang out the bait, so to speak, for a bunch of flies!" I did my buckle up with what was, I hoped, an appropriate amount of swagger.

Earl seemed to be satisfactorily impressed because he nodded and laughed and changed the topic. "C'mon. Let's get this smorg underway!" He lit the burner and proceeded to heat some water in the pot. "Give me the Beer Reconstitute packs and the rest of the bottled water we brought along."

I plopped down on the rock across from him. "How about that? Beer Reconstitute. Have you tried that before?"

"No. I saw this when I was in the MEC. Thought I'd try some."

"Meck? What's that?"

"M. E. C. It stands for Mountain Equipment Co-op. It's a huge camping and outdoor supply store." He smiled. "It's even better than a hardware store!" He handed me a cup of the reconstituted beer.

"No kidding?"

"Yeah. One time I spent a whole day in there." Earl looked at me and chuckled. "I got so busy in there that I even forgot to pick the wife up from the grocery store!"

"What did she say?"

"Nothing. She gave me her 'Silent Treatment' for three days. Yeah, the old 'Silent Treatment From The Wife'. That's not a *bad* thing, you know." He had us both laughing now.

"Yeah. I had to sleep on that saggy old couch downstairs for a couple of nights, but, well, *that's* not so bad, either. It's kinda' like camping!" We laughed again. This male bonding thing was going well. "Well, water's boiled," he announced. Open the apple pie." He poured some water into the foil packs. "There we go. We leave it sit a couple of minutes. Now for the beer." He added water to the beer pack and emptied it into our mugs.

I took a swallow from my mug and my eyes bulged. I can't remember having ever tasted anything quite so vile.

Earl had a peculiar look on his face, like he'd accidentally bitten into an extra sour lemon. His eyes squinted and they began to water.

"Good, eh?" he asked.

I must have misinterpreted his grimace. "Not really to my liking, actually." I fought the bile rising in my throat. Earl took another swallow and a pained look crossed his face. Had I been a little too blunt? I tried to soften my judgment. "It does have its own kind of flavor, I guess."

I stared at my mug for a few minutes swirling the frothy brown liquid around in it, as though that would assist in its immediate evaporation. It was no good. I could not bring myself to take another sip. I went to pour it out but Earl reached over and stopped me.

"Hey! Waste not, want not! If you're gonna' pour it *anywhere* but down your throat, you pour it in here!" and he held his mug out to me. Happy to get rid of it, I was certain that the beer would contaminate the flavor of anything else poured into that mug so I rummaged around in my pack and brought out my coffee travel mug and shook a small amount of instant Starbucks into it.

"I'll just have some coffee to wash it down with," I said and I held it out to Earl for some hot water.

Earl gazed pretty somberly at my coffee mug. "That's a goddamn big cup, Johnson."

"It was a Christmas present. The Bottomless Travel Mug."

Earl poured a tiny splash of water into it. I swear, a large thimble could have held all of the water that he gave me. I peered into the bottom of my mug. "That's all I get?"

"It's all I can give you, Johnson."

I locked eyes with him and matched his scowl.

"Well," he said a bit defensively, "we'd be here *six weeks* just boiling enough water to fill that sucker up."

I peered again into my mug. "But that's not enough water! It hardly dissolved the coffee!"

Earl was not to be budged in his water conservation decision. "Pretend it's double expresso. Conservation, Johnson! You have to have conservation in mind at all times out here. Conserve water. Conserve trees."

I sipped on my very thick coffee. "How about conserving my stomach? This is taking the conservation principle too far, I think."

Earl waved his hand around at all the trees and bushes. "You don't conserve, Johnson, next thing you know, all of this'll be gone. Now bring on the turkey and the bowls." It was clear that I would receive not an ounce more water in my cup.

Earl added a small amount of the boiled water to the turkey packages, and then he dished the apple pie into our bowls. The apple pie mixture was a pleasant surprise. I ate slowly, savoring each mouthful until my bowl was empty. I gave a satisfied belch and continued our previous conversation.

"I have a cousin who did that sort of stuff."

"What sort of stuff?"

"Environmental laws, reduced logging. All that sort of stuff."

"Really?" Earl seemed interested in my story.

"Yes. Arnold Wambacher is his name. He lives in a log cabin in B.C. He used to be an undertaker, you know. Before he ran for MLA. When he won, he switched to politics, full time."

"Ah. An undertaker and then a politician. First buried folks with dirt and now buries 'em with bullshit!"

I laughed. "A natural progression, I suppose. Well, awhile back, Arnold lobbied his party and the government to put a stop to the logging going on in the valley behind his property."

"Wanted to save the forest, did he?"

"No, what he wanted to put a stop to was the noise of the bulldozers and chainsaws that woke him up at six every morning."

"So, I'm guessing he fixed the problem?" Earl nodded as though he could empathize with cousin Arnold's dilemma.

"Not really. Now the wildlife has returned to the forest and he's got ravens cawing at five a.m. instead."

"Still better than the whine of man-made machinery, if you ask me. Up next – Turkey and Dumplings." Earl squeezed the contents of the foil packs into our bowls. "You know, speaking of wildlife, I want to show you something."

"Not pictures of your last fishing trip!"

Earl dug around in his backpack. "No. Here it is." He held up a bright yellow aerosol can that had bold black lettering on it. "We have to make sure this is in good working order."

"What's that?" I asked.

He held the can out in front of him with obvious reverence. "This here's *Bear* spray, Johnson. An intense, highly concentrated spray of cayenne and habanero peppers, actually."

Peppers? I was confused. "How does it keep bears away?"

"It doesn't keep them away, but if you have a can in your hand and you're really lucky, you can spray an attacking bear square in his face. Burns like hell and temporarily blinds him. Gives a guy a chance to run away."

"Don't you think it would be prudent to do that first?" I asked.

"Do what first?"

"Run away!"

"Johnson," Earl replied, "No man has *ever* outrun a bear."

"Is that so?" I was intrigued.

"That's so. In fact, a rule of camping of mine for *you* to remember is that *I* don't have to outrun a bear – I only have to outrun my camping partner!"

A nervous chuckle escaped from my throat, sounding more like a giggle than I had intended. "Aw-w, you're just joking! .... Aren't you?"

Earl stared at me for a second. "Of course! Anyway, this can of bear spray may someday save your life, so you should become familiar with how it works. Here."

He set his bowl down and held the can out to me. "Hold it a minute while I go take a leak. That beer really runs through a guy."

And with that, he handed me the can and disappeared into the undergrowth, leaving me with my hands wrapped around a brand new fearsome weapon.

Chapter Five

Turning the can around, I read the label.

"Contents: 55 percent crushed habanero peppers, 45 percent concentrated oil of cayenne. Use with extreme caution. Burns may result if contents come in contact with skin or mucous membranes. Harmful if swallowed. First Aid: flush skin or mucous membrane immediately with water."

So Earl thought I should become familiar with this, did he? I continued to read out loud.

"Directions for use: 1. Lift tab. 2. Hold can with spray nozzle pointed away from user. 3. Hold nozzle button down to emit spray."

I did as it directed, and pushed the button. The nozzle emitted quite a wide and even field of spray. The mechanics of it seemed easy enough. I sat the can down and took up my bowl of turkey, hoping to eat the rest of it before it got too cold.

Earl returned and sat down with a contended sigh. "That's better. Less pressure, you know?" He smiled and picked up his bowl. "Bon Appetit!" He chewed for a moment and then the yelling began.

"*Aa-ahg! Christ! Christ! Water! Water!*" He grabbed my coffee mug and drained it, and then grabbed the container of river water, gulping down several mouthfuls. And then a curious thing happened. His tongue protruded from his mouth, swollen and red.

"*What the hell happened to my food?*" he yelled.

"Nothing, I swear!"

Earl spied the can of bear spray on the ground and swooped it up. "*Did you thpray my bowl?*"

"No!" I protested.

"*Yeth you did!*" he roared.

"Not on purpose! There may have been a little spray," I confessed.

"*A little thpray?*"

"Just a little drift, that's all!"

"I oughta' drift *you!*" Earl threatened.

A cooler head had to prevail. "I was just trying out the mechanics of the can. I couldn't see where the spray went! Honest. You shouldn't have left your bowl there!"

"*I* thouldn't have left it there?"

"Well," I pointed out, "you *were* the one who set it down there, right in the way."

"*Me?*"

I had had just about enough of his childish tantrums. "Yes, you! And I had absolutely no control over *where* you put your bowl, *and I* had absolutely no control over *where* the spray would settle. So just calm down! There's no sense getting upset with me. You know, some things in the universe are just beyond our control, Earl."

I took a deep breath and tried to be reasonable. "Look at the bright side. The can has now been tested! We know that it's going to work. Here, have my supper. I don't think I can eat it. That apple pie really filled me up!" I handed him my bowl.

A peace offering.

He scowled at me for a few moments longer, and then reluctantly took my bowl. I removed a small pill bottle from my hat's lining.

Earl was still pouting. "I may never be able to thwallow properly again."

"Well," I said, "I hope you can swallow well enough to take these." I offered him two small pills.

"What're thoth? Two tableth of *Thyanide*?"

I remained calm. "As disagreeable and distressed as you are at the moment, even if I *had* cyanide, I would not *offer* it to you."

"As dithagreeable and dithtrethed as I'm feeling at the moment, if you offered it to me, *I would take it!*" Earl shouted, still worked up.

"No, no, c'mon. These are for the Gerdia."

"The what?"

"The Gerdia," I repeated.

"Giardia?" he corrected me. I thought that I detected more than just a twinge of concern in his voice.

"Yeah!" I replied. "Gee-ar-dee-a, if that's how you pronounce it. Anyway, it was probably in that untreated water that you just drank. 'Beaver Fever', I think it's called. An intestinal parasite. Causes extreme cramping and bloody diarrhea. I read about it." I tried to cheer him up. "You won't die from it though, you'll only *wish* you could! Go on." I offered the pills again. "Take them. Just crush them up in your dumplings there."

For once he did as I instructed and took the pills from my hand.

"That's how I get my cat to take pills." I said. "Stick 'em in something she likes to eat. She's kind of a cantankerous old thing, too," I added. Earl glared at me and swallowed hard.

Jeez Louise, what a grouch. Making such a big thing out of such a little deal.

I looked around our site. "Well, I suppose we'd better clean up. My turn tonight!" Earl just watched as I stood up and grabbed my backpack, producing my kitchen apron and rubber kitchen gloves. The apron was a lemon yellow and trimmed with a gathered frill.

"You know," I said, "I'm really surprised at how much stuff these packs hold. I suppose when a guy has camped as much as you have, you get used to bringing everything along."

Earl was absolutely quiet. I think that he was probably dumbfounded that *I* had thought to bring such items along. What he said next confirmed it. "Can't say that I've ever packed – that *is* an apron, isn't it?"

I poured the water from the pot on the burner into a dishpan, determined to be useful. "Yes. I threw it in at the last minute. It really isn't a good camping color though, is it? You know, if I catch on to this camping thing, I was thinking of designing a more suitable one. I mean, I think a camping apron should be, hmm ... camouflage colors and maybe have leather fringes and ... pockets! What do you think of that combination, Earl?"

"You don't really want to know ...."

I chuckled. "I'd probably be the only guy around who had one like it."

"You could bet on that."

"Hey!" I exclaimed. "Maybe I could have potholders velcro'd to the sides and I could market them! I could call them Johnson's Hot Pot Smocks! I could moonlight a new career! What do you think?"

"Don't quit your day job," Earl deadpanned. Hah! The real Earl deep down inside, I was coming to see, was such a joker.

I took the pot off the burner. "This one's clean, I guess. I'll just hang it over here to dry." The upper end of the tent pole seemed as good a place as any.

"*No-o-o!*" Earl yelled. He raced for the pot and grabbed it off the pole. "Now look at *what you've done!*" He seemed on the verge of tears as he pointed out a palm-sized hole in the tent wall.

Oops. I guess the pot was a little too hot. "I thought tents were supposed to be made out of fire proof material," I said.

"*Fire resistant! Fire resistant! Not melt-proof!*"

I examined the hole up close. "No. I guess not melt proof. Definitely not melt proof. Tell you what! I'll buy you another one at the PRIC."

"The *MEC!*" Earl exploded.

"Right! The MEC! After this weekend is over." I suddenly thought of a quick fix and dug around in my pack. "Hmm. I know that I saw it in here somewhere. Let's just string up that little tarp, right over that hole. Just to cover it up."

"There's a certain little *twerp* that *I'd* like to string up!"

Earl's sarcasm was not going to be helpful in any way at this point but I wisely chose not to point that out. "Ah ha! Here we go!" I pulled a folded nylon tarp out of the pack. I laid it over the tent top, but it just slid off. "Uh, Earl, how do we string it up?"

"Well, normally – God, 'normally' if I can use that word to describe anything around here – normally I would use the *spare* piece of rope."

"You mean the one –"

"Yeah! The one that got away!"

"Well, maybe for tonight we can just sort of lay it over the top," I suggested.

Earl seemed kind of deflated, as if his latest outburst had used up all of his energy. "You do what you can, Johnson." He shook his head, grabbed our packs, and started off into the bushes. "I'll string the packs up."

I was determined to make things right. To make Earl happy upon his return. I tried the tarp piece again.

"Hmm. Too small to cover the whole thing." I stuck my fingers through the hole and wiggled them. "The 'hole' thing!" My unintentional pun made me laugh, and then inspiration struck. I extracted a piece of strawberry gum from my hat and chewed until it was a plump, sticky wad. I divided the gum into four sections and used it to tack down each of the tarp's corners to the tent.

Another brilliant solution.

I looked over my shoulder just as Earl returned and noticed that the sun had suddenly slipped behind the mountain's top. I had fixed the tent just in time.

"Hey Earl!" I called. "Look at how dark it's getting. Should we start a campfire now?"

Earl slowly squatted down, until he was sitting on one of the flat rocks. "Actually, Johnson, I was thinking of swallowing a bottle of pain reliever and calling it a night. What do you think? I'm kinda' hurting from head to toe."

I was surprised to realize that I seemed to be enduring this trip a little better than Earl was. Maybe I was a better camper than I had thought.

"Sure, Earl. Whatever you want. You're the leader, the captain of this expedition."

Earl glanced at me. "I wonder ... can a captain mutiny *against* his crew?"

I laughed. "Ha! There you go! You've got your sense of humor back, Earl. That's great. Just before bed, too. Do you know, Gladys and I have a sign over our bed that says 'Never go to bed angry.' "

"So what do you do? Stay up and fight?"

"Hey! That's a good one! You're such a great kidder, Earl."

"It's a gift," Earl replied rather sourly.

"But seriously Earl," I said, "I want to thank you so much for this camping experience. It has been more fun than I ever imagined. How about for you?"

Earl stared at the fading strips of color in the sky and sniffed. "It's been more *something* than I ever imagined ...."

"No, really," I said. "I mean, I took first aid lessons many years ago and never had the opportunity to use my training until today. Who would have thought that we'd have needed it?"

"Yeah," Earl nodded and clenched his jaw. "Who would have thought ...."

"This whole experience really has been exciting for me," I confessed.

Earl seemed to be taking inventory as he probed his bandaged head and rubbed his shoulder, and then looked at his singed hand. Perhaps his injuries were a bit of an embarrassment to him, but he declared, "No, no. I assure you, the excitement has been all mine ...."

Once again I tried to cheer him up. "Really? Well, I'm glad I could give something back, then!" I bent over and shook his hand.

"O-o-ow!" Earl pulled his hand back.

"Whoops! Sorry! I forgot about that burn. Let me fix that hand –"

"No, no!" Earl protested, becoming the tough guy once more. "You've done enough already! Really." He motioned towards the tent. "You can be the first one in, Johnson."

Hey! I feel privileged," I said and crawled into the tent. After a few seconds, I stuck my head out. "You coming in?"

Earl grunted a little as he shifted his position on the rock. "Well, to tell you the truth, given today's events, I'm a little nervous about sleeping inside a tent where I can't get the hell away in a hurry, should the need arise."

I felt certain that Earl just needed a little confidence booster. Heck, even *I* benefitted from an ego boost every now and then. "C'mon Earl. You're the Camping Guy! You're practically indestructible!"

My compliment seemed to work. After a few seconds, Earl stood and slowly stretched.

"I suppose," he said. "Oh well, what the hell. After all, we've had quite enough activity for one day, haven't we, Johnson? I mean, Murphy's law notwithstanding, here we are tucked comfortably and *safely* away in our sleeping bags on a fine summer's night." He grabbed the can of bear spray and crawled into the tent. "What else could possibly go wrong? Right, Johnson?"

"Right, Earl," I agreed. "Good night. Sleep tight!"

"Good night Johnson," Earl yawned. He seemed to be quite worn out.

I closed my eyes and breathed deeply, willing sleep to come. However, one little detail niggled and kept me awake. I crawled out of the sleeping bag and unzipped the tent.

"*Now* where are you going?" Earl asked.

"My turn to go for a leak," I replied.

Earl handed me the can. "Here. Take the bear spray with you."

"Right! I'll be right back." I stumbled away in the dark, choosing to stop a modest distance away from the tent.

From where I stood, relieving myself, I could hear Earl call out.

"Johnson? Johnson! That you? Johnson! What the hell are you wiggling the tent for?"

Wiggling the tent? No, it certainly wasn't me. I hurried back.

"*Oh, my God!*" The most horrifying scene was playing out in front of me.

There was Earl, standing in a semi-crouch, facing our tent, axe in hand. And facing him, from just behind our flimsy wall of nylon material and flexible poles was an enormous, growling bear, a shredded piece of tarp hanging from its drooling jaws. Apparently it had just enjoyed the remains of my strawberry gum. Panic-stricken, I was frozen to the spot until Earl's voice broke through my cocoon of fear.

"*Run, Johnson! RUN!*"

And so I did. I ran like I had never run before. I ran until I collapsed, unable to will my legs to take another step.

And there it was. Our meeting place.

I crawled between two large boulders and tucked my useless legs under me. My chest was burning and I gasped for air. I counted my ragged breaths and I waited for Earl.

Chapter Six

It was almost two years after that camping trip before I finally felt ready to return to those mountains.

I had learned a lot about myself on that weekend, and even more about Earl, a guy I had just met.

I had my own equipment now. I liked to think that I was carrying on Earl's tradition. I liked to think that he was still living on the edge, and maybe even that from time to time, he and his boy were peeking down over that edge at me.

I didn't have strong convictions about the afterlife but just in case he was listening from that place somewhere beyond, I held up a small plastic bag that was filled with stuff that would have looked like ordinary food chunks to anyone else, but I knew that Earl would understand.

I held it up against that beautiful clear sky, framed by those majestic mountains, and took a slow, deep breath. Earl had been right. I could feel the peace of nature all around me.

"Hey Earl!" I called softly. "I'm still working on that bacon and egg thing."

The End.

ACKNOWLEDGMENTS

My thanks goes out to my husband, Mike, for his keen editorial skills and for his suggestions for fine tuning the storyline during the conversion process from its original form of a one act play into its present short story form.

I am also grateful to Deb Widmer, Shirley Nordlund, Vivienne MacNeil, and Catherine Millard, my beta readers, for their attention to detail and willingness to provide input into *The Camping Guy*.

Many thanks as well go to my cover designer, Derek Murphy, at Creativindie Covers, for his wonderful skill in producing the delightful cover for *The Camping Guy*.

And most of all, I extend my heartfelt gratitude to Norman and Hazel Lavoy, and to Mike Greenlay for their early participation in bringing *The Camping Guy* to life.

ABOUT THE AUTHOR

Born and raised on the Canadian prairies, Dianne Greenlay saves lives by day (as well as being an author, she is a physiotherapist in a remote sole charge clinic and a retired EMT), and she tells lies by night (as any entertaining fiction writer would do).

Greenlay is also a playwright and Creative Director of a long-running community theatre group, Darkhorse Theatre. However her biggest achievement is having successfully raised a family of six children in a home with only one bathroom (and everyone got out alive.)

Besides being the author of *The Camping Guy*, which is available as both a one-act script and a short story, Greenlay is the multiple award-winning author of the swashbuckling adventure novels, *Quintspinner – A Pirate's Quest*, and *Deadly Misfortune*.

Dianne Greenlay is fluent in at least her mother tongue and she thanks her fierce English teachers for that. More of her thoughts on life can be found at www.diannegreenlay.com .

Quintspinner – A Pirate's Quest
(An Excerpt)

The knife felt strangely familiar.

Its handle lay heavy and warm in William's hand. The strange double curved blade had, at the moment of its birth in the fires of a skilled but long-forgotten smith, been forged as an extension of the metal handle and now, as William's fingers curled around it, it nestled solidly in the palm of his hand.

A perfect fit.

It was unlike any skinning or hunting knife he had ever handled. Plain and darkened with a deep grey tarnish, it had been overlooked by the rest of the crew, bypassed in favor of the more ornate and lengthy weapons. William had found it at the bottom of the *Mary Jane's* arms chest.

Perhaps it had been considered by the others to be too small to be safely used in hand to hand combat, too dangerously diminutive to be pitched against a sailor's preferred weapon such as a cutlass or boarding axe, and thus it had been left behind. To William, however, it would be perfect in such a fight.

Perfect to be launched from a distance.

From a practiced hand.

Or from either hand, he smiled to himself. *Now to fashion a sheath for such a thing. Perhaps the bos'n will not miss a small amount of sail and thread.*

Lost in his thoughts of the logistics of obtaining materials for such a casing, William descended into the lower levels of the ship, intending to smuggle a small amount of cloth from the hold. His new weapon had a comfortable weight to it, its surface slick and smooth, its shaft feeling well balanced against the mass of its handle.

Overcome with a totally impetuous desire to test its behavior in flight, William hurled his dagger, aiming for the corner of a wooden box stored in the shadows at the base of the galley wall. With a spontaneous flick of his wrist, he sent it spinning on a short trajectory path. It found its mark landing with a satisfying thud as the tip bit deeply into the box.

William stared in distress.

Only a hair's breadth away from his knife, a hand froze in mid-reach.

A delicate hand that had come out of the shadow without warning, apparently seeking the same box. William sucked his breath in sharply as his eyes, now adjusted to the low light, came to rest on the blue ring, glowing ever so faintly even in the semidarkness.

God Almighty! What have I done!

He opened his mouth to utter an apology, an explanation, anything at all, but all that exited from his throat was a ragged breath.

Tess stepped out of the shadow and fixed him in her stare. William was sure she could hear the panic in the hammering rhythm of his own heart. For a few tortuous heartbeats neither of them spoke, and then Tess took a deep breath.

"What were you aiming for?" she inquired, her voice steady and low.

"Miss Willoughby! I am so sorry! I didn't see anybody around and I didn't know that you were reaching for it! It was inexcusable and–"

"What was your target?" she cut in, her voice just as calm as William's was frantic.

"Uh … the corner of the box, Miss," and he nodded miserably in its general direction.

Tess peered down at the box and spoke out loud, though William was not sure that it was for his benefit at all.

"My gran–Mrs. Hanley requested that I bring some dried sprigs of mint to her for use against the malodorous air in sick bay." She grasped her ring with the fingers of her free hand, absentmindedly toying with it, or perhaps just hiding it from his eyes. William was not sure which.

"I had been momentarily confused about opening the box. In the dark I was not sure it was the one I sought, therefore I hesitated before reaching out."

She bent forward again, squatting beside the box, and ran her fingers along the knife blade and handle.

"Well Sir, it appears that you have found your intended mark indeed." She looked up at William and smiled. "No harm done at all then, as *I* was aiming for its latch. Do you often hit your mark dead on?"

"Nearly always," William sputtered, "But Miss, I am sick to think of what could – what might have happened ...." His voice trailed away.

"What do you propose you do to make it up to me then?"

"Truthfully, I have no idea but I assure you that I am at your service, Miss! No request from you would go unanswered."

"None?" Tess's smile had been replaced by a stern look, desirous of his affirmation.

"I assure you that."

"Then ...." She stepped forward and drew herself up as tall as she could. The nearness of her once again made William's breath harsh. He stared into her eyes; even by lantern light they were as deeply green as the ocean they sailed upon. For a few powerful heartbeats they stood, their faces mere inches apart.

God provides the birds with food, but He does not drop it into their nests. Make what you can of your given opportunities.

Seemingly out of nowhere, Captain Crowell's words whispered inside William's head nudging, taunting, and suddenly he felt their hidden meaning open up to him.

Impetuously, he reached out, his hands resting on the slight swells of her hips, his fingers drawing her against him. There was no hesitation in those emerald eyes. William bent his head forward and lightly brushed Tess's lips with his own, then pulled back and searched her face. Her eyes were half closed, the contours of her face beautiful even in the shadows of the dim light. Her body pressed against him.

He kissed her again, this time tasting her lips, meeting the gentle tip of her tongue with his own.

He alternately licked and suckled her skin, trailing butterfly kisses gently down the front of her throat, the tip of his tongue stopping to swirl enticingly in the dip above her collarbone.

Tess's lips parted as she tilted her head back and a soft moan escaped her. Her breath came in shallow waves as she drank in the sensations he was causing. Lost in a moment of lustful madness, William kissed her again, and felt her hands slide up around his neck. Her touch upon his skin was thrilling, so overpowering ... and *quite* wonderful.

She responded to him, leaning into him, caressing his face with her fingertips. She felt the short stubble on his skin, and then slowly outlined his cheekbones, drawing her fingers along to track the angle of his jaw. Her touch was electrifying and William groaned with the pleasure of it.

"What was it that you wanted to ask me?" he whispered hopefully, nuzzling her neck just below her ear.

"Hmmm?" Tess exhaled. "I–I wanted to ask you to teach me … to throw as you do. With a weapon of my own."

Her words sent an instant chill through William, squelching the heat of the moment.

He pulled away from her and his eyes widened. *Does she know what she asks of me?* To teach a woman to use a hand weapon, here on a ship would be a forbidden thing, he was sure of it. *Probably a lashing, or worse if I'm caught! It would have to be done in secret, and how would that look, if anyone discovered us together?*

And then the reality of being together, of what they were doing–had just done–the reality of being together under these far more treacherous circumstances washed over him.

What in the bejeezes hell am I doing? he cursed himself. Not that he regretted having Tess in his arms. It was the sudden realization of the danger that his own actions had put her in, as well as himself, that made him feel shaky and sick to his stomach.

And her already being betrothed! If her miserable fiancé were to catch us, we'd both be thrown overboard! How could I have put my own desires ahead of her safety? To have put her secure future into jeopardy? And now, to do as she asks?

To teach her to throw?

William looked into Tess's face. It was full of steely resolve.

He saw no hope for himself.

If he didn't agree to her terms, and she were to tell anyone of his rash behavior, knife or otherwise, he would be severely punished, most likely ending in a long-drawn out and painful death. Of that he was certain.

Deadly Misfortune

(An Excerpt)

The man stared at the woman, momentarily caught off guard.

She sat upon the ground, her torso resting against the moss covered tree trunk, and his eyes roved over her.

Such perfection. Attractive face with small nose and plump lips parted slightly as though poised to speak. Cinnamon skin dappled from the filtered sunlight in an intriguing pattern of tawny, dark, and gold. Thick tendrils of coal black hair curling softly over her bare shoulders, her breasts defiant and full in their youthfulness.

Perfect.

Except for the musket ball hole blasted squarely into her shattered breastbone.

He blinked in surprise. Catching his breath, the hunter dropped into a crouch as he slid back into the protective camouflage of the jungle's foliage. He reassessed the scene, his heart pounding, all senses on full alert.

Damn it! He cursed this part of his job. *Competition. Incompetent fools!* He was the best– everybody knew it–and if he had found this pretty little Maroon first, he'd still have her to collect the bounty on. *An' make no mistake about it, the bounty on this one woulda' been worth plenty, that's fer sure.*

His annoyance at such a loss edged him towards a full-fledged temper fit. *I coulda' kept her fer a little fun myself, fer awhile anyways! Shit! What the bejeezes happened here? She ain't even armed. She escaped with nothin' more than the rags on her back. What a total waste!*

He shook his head. What was there to salvage? He'd tracked someone, *something*, from the plantation in the lower land, up through this godforsaken hothouse–*who knew it was gonna be so damned hot this far up the mountain*–for nearly a full day, following subtle signs through the misery of clouds of biting insects and, in his haste, brushing up against clusters of poisonous leaves that had caused his hands and arms to blister, only to come upon this disaster.

He peered over at her corpse. Now all that he had to show for his time and effort was the tiny scrap of a baby still cradled in the crook of her lifeless arm.

Mewing brat! That was what had drawn him in this direction in the first place, only a heartbeat before the sound of the musket blast.

An' that sucklin' ain't gonna' last long neither, he grumbled to himself. Unless he could find a wet nurse back at the sugar mill, there wouldn't be a hope in hell. The thing would starve. And if it didn't quit bawling right now, he might just have to put it out of its misery himself.

He squinted over at the baby, its tiny mouth stretched open in a primitive howl. And then he saw it.

The sole of a boot.

Tension crackled through him, the shock of his discovery hitting hard. No Maroon, this body. The boot's leather had been shaped by a reasonably skilled cobbler. Its style practically shouted 'bounty hunter' to him. His rival probably. He frowned, his forehead wrinkling up in confusion.

What the hell happened?

Cautiously emerging from his hiding place, he stepped forward for a closer look and squinted down at his newest discovery. His eyes suddenly bulged with comprehension, the hairs on the back of his neck prickling with fear. His rival's shirt collar was wrapped around a bloodied stump of a neck, the slain hunter's head nowhere in sight. He had only a moment to consider this as the swish of a machete blade closed in around him.

The sharp blow to his neck felled him and he pitched forward, dead before his own body crashed down upon the corpse at his feet.

***

Laying down his machete, and repositioning the baby boy in the dead woman's arm, Jacko held the infant in place while the child nursed greedily for what would be the last time at his mother's breast.

When at last the child's belly was sufficiently full, Jacko dipped a moistened finger into a leather satchel tied at his waist. He slipped the powdered fingertip into the baby's mouth, feeling the reflexive tug of the baby's sucking. The calming effect of the powder was nearly immediate and he wrapped the now sluggish child in a chest sling, before turning his attention to the young woman's body.

Glancing at the clotting wound in her chest, white-hot grief stabbed him in his own, and for a moment he clenched his eyes shut, dizzy with the effort to suppress his rage. Taking deep breaths, he forced himself to concentrate on the task at hand.

It would not do to have any bodies found so close to the secret village. The bounty hunters had nearly discovered the small encampment of Maroons, only another valley away from here.

Making a separate trip with each head and a corpse, he dragged them deeper into the undergrowth. Limping heavily with the exertion, he recalled his own near death during an attack from a bounty hunter. The flesh on his thigh and buttock had never fully recovered from the gunshot and knife wounds he had suffered at the hands of such a man, although he had miraculously lived through his injuries.

Had it not been for his mate's potions and prayers to the gods, and the healing powers of the white woman who called herself Tess, Jacko knew he would have been just another body left to feed the jungle's spirits.

He breathed up a prayer of thanks and a request for continued safety for himself and the village's people, before rolling each set of body and head down into a steep crevice at the bottom of a narrow ravine. Not even the dogs would be able to track the missing slave hunters any further.

And they *would* come, he knew. With more trackers. They always did.

Returning finally to the remaining body, he bent down and gathered the woman in his arms. Holding her close, her child between them, he nuzzled her cheek with his own, inhaling deeply in an effort to capture her scent one last time. His nostrils flared and the crushing grief returned, scalding him as it bored deeper into his chest.

She smelled only of death.

Her spirit had left the body, but would be hovering nearby, he thought, waiting for the appropriate rituals to be performed by Mambo. Without those, her spirit could not be set completely free from the physical body, and it would be forced to roam in the darkness of night forever.

Mambo, his mate, would know what to do to ensure that would not happen. She would ensure that this woman would not suffer such a fate.

Mambo would release their daughter's soul.

With a heart that was as heavy as the body he now carried across his shoulders, Jacko staggered deeper into the foliage and up towards the hidden village. His sorrow drilled into his chest, morphing with every breath into a focused rage.

It was time.

17779533R00059

Made in the USA
Charleston, SC
28 February 2013